The Berenstain Bears and TOO MUCH BIRTHDAY

A FIRST TIME BOOK®

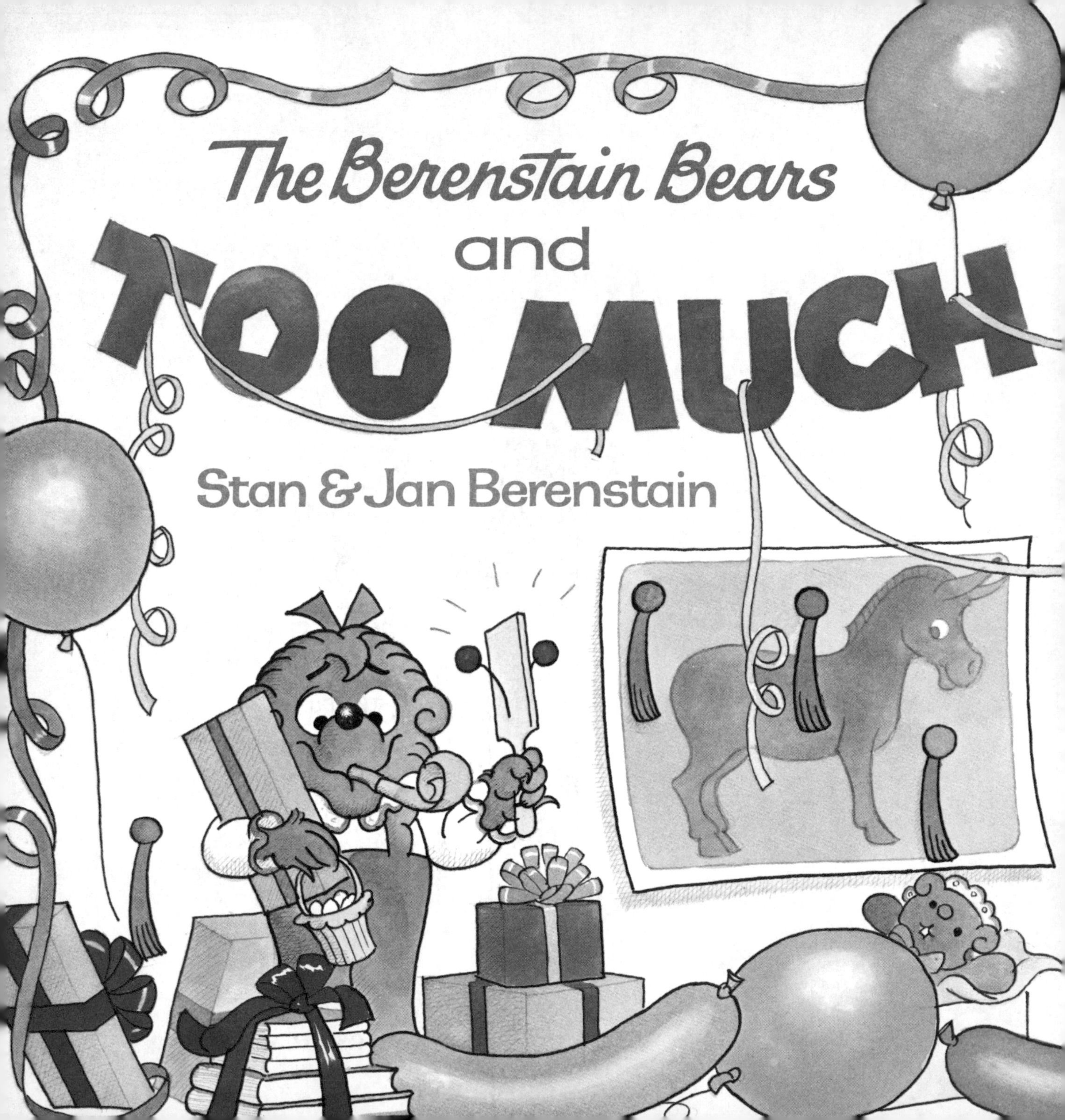
The Berenstain Bears
and
TOO MUCH
Stan & Jan Berenstain

Random House New York

Published in the United States by Random House Children's Books,
a division of Random House, Inc., New York.
Random House and the colophon are registered trademarks of
Random House, Inc. First Time Books and the colophon are registered trademarks
of Berenstain Enterprises, Inc.
randomhouse.com/kids BerenstainBears.com
Library of Congress Cataloging-in-Publication Data
Berenstain, Stan. The Berenstain bears and too much birthday. (A First time book)
Summary: Sister Bear is distressed that things don't go quite right
at her birthday party. ISBN 978-0-394-87332-9 (trade)
[1. Bears—Fiction. 2. Birthdays—Fiction. 3. Parties—Fiction.]
I. Berenstain, Jan. II. Title. III. Series: Berenstain, Stan. First time books.
PZ7.B4483Beln 1986 [E] 85-14529
Printed in the United States of America
65 64 63 62 61 60 59

It was a bright, beautiful, early September day in Bear Country. Mama Bear had harvested the last of the season's pumpkins and was piling them high in her wheelbarrow when she heard Papa's distant warning call: *"Timber-r-r!"* The call meant that he had felled another tree.

"I do hope Papa and the cubs are being careful," she said.

CR-R-RASH! went the tree as it fell to the forest floor. Woodsbear Papa was always careful about his work. He had cut the tree just-so with his great saw. Then he and the cubs stood back and watched it fall into a bed of brush that Brother and Sister had prepared.

HAPPY BI
R

“Look!” said Sister when the dust and leaves had settled. “It has rings!”

“Yes,” said Brother. “Sort of like the ripples in a pond when you throw in a stone!”

“Those are annual rings,” explained Papa. “They tell us how old the tree is.”

Sister started to count, but she got stuck at twelve. Brother took over and finished the count: "...twenty-five, twenty-six, twenty-seven! Wow! This tree is twenty-seven years old!"

"That's a lot older than I am," said Sister.

"It sure is!" said Brother, laughing. "You're only five."

"Five going on six!" said Sister. Brother was eight and it annoyed her that however old she got, she never caught up with him. It didn't seem quite fair.

"Do *we* have annual rings, Papa?" Sister asked.

"No," said Papa, giving her a little hug. "We have something even better—birthdays! *And birthday parties!* And it seems to me," he continued, "that you're having a birthday pretty soon."

"Am I going to have a party?" cried Sister, jumping up and down with excitement. "A birthday party with all the trimmings?" Brother was excited too.

"I don't see why not," said Papa. "Six is a pretty important birthday."

The cubs got so excited that they took turns shouting:

"A real party with cake and ice cream?"

"And decorations?"

"And favors?"

"And games?"

"Hmm," said Mama when they got back home. "A birthday party? Yes, six years old calls for a little celebration. I suppose we could manage a nice, quiet little party."

But a nice, quiet little party wasn't what Sister, Brother, and Papa had in mind. What they had in mind was a *big, noisy, exciting* party with—

lots and lots of guests,

oodles of goodies,

games, games, games,

wall-to-wall decorations,

piles of fancy presents,

and a fabulous birthday cake.

"But let's not get carried away," said Mama. "You know, there's such a thing as 'too much birthday.'"

"Too much birthday!" scoffed Papa and the cubs. "How could you ever have too much birthday?"

Mama just sighed and hoped she would be able to keep things under control.

But it wasn't long before she forgot her worries and began to go along with the excitement....

The guest list got longer and longer.

The birthday cake got bigger and fancier.

The party goods
and goodies piled up
higher and higher.

Papa and the cubs
decorated the tree house
inside *and* out.

And on the big day Mama even gave Sister her present early—a beautiful frilly blouse—so she could wear it to the party.

"Oh, good!" said Papa. "The ponies and the merry-go-round are here."

"The *what* are here?" cried Mama.

"Didn't I mention it?" Papa said. "I rented ponies and a merry-go-round for the party!"

The cubs were very excited—especially Sister! What a party this was going to be!

At three o'clock sharp the guests began to arrive. They greeted Sister, piled up their presents, and joined the fun.

The first game was Going to Jerusalem. You play it by going around and around, and the one that's caught on the rug when the music stops is out. It was lots of fun—except that Sister was the first one out.

Then they played
Spin the Bottle,
which was lots of fun too—except that
Sister was so shy she wouldn't kiss
anybody but Brother, and all the cubs
laughed and teased.

Pin the Tail on the Donkey was different. Sister stuck a tail on just the right spot.

But of course she couldn't win the prize—it was her party...and it wouldn't be polite.

Then they gave out the favors. Sister got a party pipe and tickled her friend Freddy's nose. Freddy got a trick plastic flower that squirted water all over Sister's birthday blouse.

The ponies and the merry-go-round were a big success—except that Sister had sampled so many party goodies that she got a little sick from all the up-and-down and round-and-round.

At last it was time to bring out the birthday cake and blow out the six candles. Sister took a deep breath and blew as hard as she could…

—and not a single candle went out!

"That's how many cubs you're going to have when you grow up!" shouted her friends, teasing her with the old superstition. After a lot of blowing, though, she finally blew out all the candles and everybody cheered and sang "Happy Birthday."

That's when Mama noticed a big tear beginning to roll down Sister's cheek. By the time the song was over, she was crying so loud you could hardly hear the singing.

"Sweetie!" said Mama. "What's the matter?"

"It isn't fair!" Sister said between sobs. "I was the first one out in Going to Jerusalem! I don't like kissing games! I didn't get the donkey game prize! Freddy squirted my new blouse! And I don't *want* to have six cubs—I only want to have three!" And then she began to cry again.

WA-A-A-A-A-A!

"Don't you want to open your presents?" asked her friends, crowding around. Well, there's nothing like opening up a pile of lovely presents to cheer you up, and after a while she was herself again.

Then, after cake and
ice cream, her friends wished
her Happy Birthday and left.

Sister sighed a big sigh,
then climbed up onto Papa's lap.

"Thank you for my birthday party," she said.

Papa smiled and said, "Parties *are* exciting and presents *are* lovely, but Mama was right—the important thing is that you're going to be six for a whole year and it's up to you to make the most of it—to learn, to have fun, to grow in every way."

"Say," she said, "I wonder how much I've grown since my last birthday!"

“Let’s find out,”
suggested Papa.

“Wow!” said Brother.
“A whole inch and
a half!”

“And speaking of growth,” said Mama, “here’s a school paper you did in kindergarten—and here’s one you just did in first grade.” There was quite a difference.

“And here are two of your paintings,” said Brother. “One from last year and one from this year.”

It was true. Sister had come a long way since she was five.

And now that she was six, Papa announced that she was going to be allowed to stay up later—a whole half-hour later.

"Wow! A whole half-hour!" said Sister proudly.

But the way it turned out, Sister Bear was so tired from "too much birthday" that she couldn't even stay up until her old bedtime. She was sound asleep when Papa carried her up to bed.

"And how old are you today?" asked Papa when she woke up the next morning.

"Six," said Sister. And then, grinning from ear to ear, "Six going on seven!"

HAPPY BI
R